Angela Bremner

PUFFIN BOOKS

HIDE TILL DAYTIME

It was at the very end of an exhausting day's shopping when the Pepper children got lost. Their father was already cross about the expense and missing a day at the office, and their mother was tired, so when four-year-old George upset the honey in the Food Hall and all the angry faces and voices started closing in, Agatha knew it would be the very last straw.

Without thinking about it, she grabbed George and hustled him as far away as she could, where it seemed quiet and safe. 'I'll take you to Mummy as soon as I've washed the honey off you,' she said sensibly, but by the time the honey was cleaned off and they crept nervously downstairs again, the store was closed and their parents had gone home without them.

To be locked up for the night in a huge dark building was very scary indeed, especially if you had a tearful little brother to take care of. Agatha felt cold all over, and a lost, hollow feeling started creeping up from her middle, but later on, when she discovered they were well and truly locked in for the night, she heard the stealthy footsteps creeping up on her in the dark, and then she was near the edge of panic!

This is a riveting adventure story about a very brave little girl, for throughout everything that happened Agatha really did manage to keep her head and to look after George, and only she knew how much courage that took.

Joan Phipson was born in 1912 in Australia. She has travelled widely, including England and India. She is married, with two children, and lives 180 miles outside Sydney breeding sheep and cattle.

JOAN PHIPSON

Hide Till Daytime

Illustrated by Mary Dinsdale

PUFFIN BOOKS

PUFFIN BOOKS

Published by the Penguin Group
27 Wrights Lane, London w8 5TZ, England
Viking Penguin Inc., 40 West 23rd Street, New York, New York 10010, USA
Penguin Books Australia Ltd, Ringwood, Victoria, Australia
Penguin Books Canada Ltd, 2801 John Street, Markham, Ontario, Canada L3R 1B4
Penguin Books (NZ) Ltd, 182–190 Wairau Road, Auckland 10, New Zealand

Penguin Books Ltd, Registered Offices: Harmondsworth, Middlesex, England

First published by Hamish Hamilton Children's Books Ltd 1977
Published in Puffin Books 1979
Reprinted 1982, 1984, 1986, 1987, 1988

Made and printed in Great Britain by
Richard Clay Ltd, Bungay, Suffolk
Set in Linotype Pilgrim

Chapter One

BECAUSE it was winter the streets were already dark when the Pepper family arrived at the David Jones Market Street store in Sydney. A flood of yellow light was pouring out of the big entrance doors. A flood of people was pouring out, too, for it was nearly closing time. Agatha had hoped she was on her way home as well. It had been a nasty day. She hated being made to try on clothes. And George, who was four and should have known better, had kicked the sales lady in the face when she had tried to put a shoe on his foot. Their father kept saying he should not have taken the day off from work. Their mother kept saying it was only once a year and they were his children weren't they. Every so often their father looked at all the parcels and said he didn't know he was sure where all the money was to come from.

Mrs Pepper stopped dead at the entrance doors. Then she said, 'I'll have to buy something for our dinner. There won't be time to cook anything.' Before Mr Pepper could stop her – and he tried – she was away

down the stairs into the Food Hall and they all had to
follow in case they lost her in the crowd. There was
some danger of George being swept out of the doors
again by shoppers hurrying home and Mr Pepper said
to Agatha, 'You hold George's hand. Look after him in
case he gets lost. You're nine now.' He said it quite
crossly, as if it were all Agatha's fault. Then he went
hurrying off in front, for he could still just see the top
of Mrs Pepper's head.

Agatha snatched George's hand. She expected it to be sticky and it was. She pushed her way through the people, dragging George after her. The people didn't like it when she bumped into them. But she dared not lose sight of her father, and it was true that she was nine. Even so, she could not yet see over the tops of grown-ups' heads. Having to peer under elbows and round the waists of plump ladies made it difficult for her to keep him in sight.

At last she saw that her father had caught up with her mother. They were standing together by the counter where the chickens were being roasted. She hoped her mother was buying one. They smelled so delicious. But she saw that they were arguing again. She was sure it would be about the money.

George had been banged about among the people's knees and he didn't like it. He began to make roaring noises. Agatha knew this would make her father angrier still, so she waited with George a little way off. She kept her eyes fixed on her parents, determined not to lose them. She knew they could not see her because of the crowd of people in between. So far Mr Pepper had not heard George, though some other people had and were looking at him hard. Agatha kept his hand behind her back, pretending he did not belong to her.

Mr and Mrs Pepper seemed to have come to some kind of agreement, for Agatha saw her mother lean

forward over the counter and say something to the lady behind it. Her father stood back with his lips pressed close together and a frown wrinkling his eyebrows. They were going to have a chicken after all. She knew that wrapping it would take a little time so she allowed herself to look away. She found that she and George were standing in front of a big transparent container which said, HONEY. It was high up on the shelf and the light was gleaming through the honey. There was a tap at the bottom of the container and the shop assistant was busy bending over it, holding a cardboard mug under the tap and letting a golden stream of honey run into it. A lady with a lot of large parcels was standing beside her, looking impatiently at the golden stream. But honey is as leisurely as a summer day and it was going in at its own pace.

For the moment Agatha had forgotten George. But now his roars grew suddenly louder. He had seen his parents over at the chicken counter. The lunge forward that he made nearly pulled Agatha off her feet. In a sudden rage she jerked him back. Afterwards she knew she would not have pulled him so hard if she had not been angry. He flew backwards, lost his balance and before she could do anything about it he had banged into the impatient lady and her parcels. The lady was not expecting to be bumped into by anybody, and George caught her behind the knees. She stumbled forward and lurched into the shop assistant holding the mug of honey. The mug shot out of her hand and on to George, who was now on his back at her feet. He was also directly under the slowly flowing stream of honey that came from the tap. Agatha saw the lady grab at her parcels, saw her lose her grip of her basket and saw the parcels tumble out. One of them split open. A white cloud of flour burst from it, filling the air with fog and settling on George, who had decided to have one more roar before getting to his feet. The flour stuck to the honey and sent him white in patches.

Everyone began suddenly talking at once. Their voices were loud, high and shrill. Agatha heard the words, '– parents should be charged – If they were mine – spanking – Superintendent –' and without even thinking what she did she dragged George to his feet, slipped off her raincoat, wrapped it round him and pulled him away. She did not know where to go, but there was a cluster of people not far off and she joined them, knowing that once among the waists, elbows and knees, she and George would be hard to find.

The cluster of people was at the foot of the escalator, and in a moment she found that she and George were being swept away, up to the next floor. It was not what she had expected, but it was a wonderful way to escape. For a fleeting second she looked over the rail and saw the shop assistant and the lady, still talking hard. Their faces were quite red and they both kept turning and looking all round them. A sea of honey and flour was spreading over the floor.

Agatha could think of only one thing. She and George must escape from the lady who wanted to

charge her mother and father. The shop assistant would be after them too. Perhaps soon the entire staff of David Jones would be hunting them. Her father's words, 'You're nine now,' kept ringing in her head. She was nine, and she had flung George into the honey. It was all her fault. She wished that the escalator would blow up under her, or that the roof would suddenly fall in. But they arrived safely at the top. She would have liked to ride on up the escalator for ever, but there was no alternative but to step off. The idea of going on up remained in her mind. She flew round to where the lifts were. George, with his feet almost off the ground, was dragged along behind. He looked quite respectable inside Agatha's raincoat and the funny feeling of the honey inside it made him forget to roar. He was silent and unnoticeable as they melted into another group of people. This group was on the point of stepping into the lift. They were late, anxious, and not disposed to notice a white-faced girl and a silent boy who smelt of honey.

Again they were borne aloft. They were the last to leave the lift. The lift man gave them a funny look and said, 'This is as far as we go.'

Agatha pretended not to notice the look, but said loudly, 'This is where we have to meet Mummy. Come on, George.' And she stepped out of the lift.

She got George out too without trouble because he had brightened at the thought of meeting his mother again. They stood still while the lift doors shut behind them. Agatha pretended to be looking for her mother.

Up here the shop was strangely silent. All the shoppers seemed to have left. There was no one near them

at all. If they were being hunted for, the hunt had not come this way so far.

All round them were things for sale, arranged invitingly for people to look at. There were groups of garden furniture. White chairs surrounded solid outdoor tables. Brightly-coloured garden umbrellas were poised above them – all waiting, it seemed to Agatha, for someone to come and sit down. Farther off were refrigerators, washing machines, egg-beaters, irons, all ready to go into someone's home and be cared for. All the way down the floor under the bright lights were parts of people's houses, waiting to be bought. But as far as Agatha could see there was not a soul to buy them. At this end of the floor nothing moved at all.

'Where's Mummy?' said George loudly.

'Sh!' Agatha swung round and almost clapped her hand over his mouth. But there was no one to hear and George, now she came to study him closely, looked quite forlorn. Her raincoat hung about him, sticking here and there to his body, and there was a shining smear of honey all over one cheek. It seemed to have escaped the flour and glistened stickily from eye to chin. She was no longer angry with him. She had to look after him and she knew what she had to do.

'I'll take you to Mummy,' she said, 'as soon as I've washed the honey off you.'

'I want to go now,' said George.

She saw his bottom lip crinkle up and said quickly, 'Come on. There must be a bathroom somewhere. We'll hurry.' She took his hand again. It was stickier than ever because of the honey that had run down his arm.

Chapter Two

DOWN in the Food Hall beside the chicken roaster Mrs Pepper was holding out the money, waiting for the shop assistant to take it and give her the chicken she had chosen. Mr Pepper was standing on one side of the queue that had formed behind Mrs Pepper. She had taken rather a long time deciding which chicken she would have. Mr Pepper kept looking at his watch. He was being pushed farther and farther away from Mrs Pepper by desperate last-minute shoppers. At last he said loudly, 'Frances, I'll have to go. I must get back to the office before it shuts.'

Everyone in the queue looked round and Mrs Pepper looked round, too. She thought it was the last straw to be deserted at such a crucial moment. 'All right,' she said crossly. 'But please take the children.' A man with an enormous vacuum cleaner passed just as she said the last three words and she had to shout them loudly.

But Mr Pepper was now too far away to hear her clearly, and all he understood were the last three shouted words – TAKE THE CHILDREN. So he nodded

hard to show he understood, and Mrs Pepper looked over her shoulder just in time to see him nod and his mouth form the words again – TAKE THE CHILDREN.

So, having said, 'You'll take the children, then,' and seeing Mrs Pepper appear to understand, he hurried off, his mind already full of other things.

Mrs Pepper heaved a sigh of relief as she handed over the money. She would get home much quicker if she did not have the children with her. Perhaps she would even have dinner ready by the time they got back. So she took the chicken and walked out of the shop a little way behind Mr Pepper.

Chapter Three

AGATHA had a feeling she would find a bathroom in one of the corners of the floor. So she led George up the shop along one side, past a row of painted wooden wardrobes. Suddenly from somewhere ahead of her there came the sound of voices. Then footsteps. They were getting louder – coming towards her. Someone must have been looking for them on this floor after all. She squeezed George's hand tight and looked about for somewhere to hide. There were the wardrobes, right beside her. She pulled him over to the nearest one and after a minute's fumbling, found she could slide the door back quite easily.

'We'll just wait in here a minute, George,' she said, and hoped he would not decide to roar again. She pushed him in, climbed in behind him and quickly slid the door across. It was dark, and smelt pleasantly of raw wood. The voices were growing louder and the footsteps were clearly coming towards them. There seemed to be several people. She had her hand ready to press over George's mouth if he began to make a noise.

But he stayed silent as a mouse and she knew that she loved him after all.

The voices and footsteps came, passed the line of wardrobes and began to fade. When they had quite died away Agatha began to slide the door back very slowly. She had only opened it a crack when she heard more voices. They seemed to be coming towards her, too, so she quickly slid the door shut again. She heard the voices and she heard the footsteps. She could not quite catch what the people were talking about, although she listened hard. She very much wanted to know if they were looking for her and George. They approached, passed the wardrobe and faded as the last ones had done. And George beside her was quite still and silent. But she did not dare open the door again for a long time.

When she did – an inch at a time – it was to find that once again there was not a soul in sight. Some of the lights were out now and the floor was as silent as a church. She stepped out, one foot at a time, and looked round to make sure George followed. Then she saw why he had been so quiet. He was sitting on the floor of the wardrobe. He had opened the front of her raincoat and was contentedly licking the honey and flour off his clothes.

'Come on,' she said. 'I'll give you a nice wash and then we'll find Mummy.'

They walked all round the floor, cautiously at first, and without talking. But there was no one there. It was quite empty now, and there was no bathroom. They went back towards the lifts and escalators, but the escalators had stopped. Agatha and George peered down the long row of shining metal steps to the floor below. It was still lit up, and they could hear people moving about and vacuum cleaners going. Agatha pulled George back quickly and turned to the lifts. Their indicators were blank and dark. No lifts seemed to be moving. For a moment she wondered if there was no way down except into the arms of the cleaners below. Then she noticed an opening in the wall at the corner to the left of the lifts. She led George towards it, went through and found that they were at the top of a flight of concrete stairs. In front of her there was another opening from the landing and through it she saw the corner of a basin. There, beside the stairs, was a bathroom at last. She was so pleased to have found both stairs and bathroom that she said cheerfully, 'Come on, Georgie. Now we shan't be long. Then we'll go down to Mummy. I expect she'll be waiting for us.'

Chapter Four

SURE enough, there were rows of basins, plenty of soap and paper towels. When she tried the water she was pleased to find it was still hot. She peeled off the raincoat, which had stuck again, and washed the honey off it first. Then she attacked George himself. He stood in front of the basin, half glistening with honey, half white with flour and his mouth smeared with both flour and honey, and Agatha began to giggle. 'Georgie, if you could see yourself,' she said at last.

But George was beginning to feel both uncomfortable and cold, and in a moment he was going to cry. Agatha filled the basin with warm water and began to work on him. It took a long time, far longer than she thought. But once she had begun there was no stopping. By the time she had finished he was wet all down the front, but most of the sticky had gone. She wrapped her raincoat round him again, gave him a kiss on the cheek, partly to see if it was still sticky, and said, 'Come on, now. We'll go downstairs to Mummy.' He looked so much more respectable that she was quite pleased with herself.

They went to the top of the stairs and looked down. The flights were still lighted, but it was all very quiet and there seemed to be no one about. Hand in hand they began to go down. Agatha was as silent as she could be, but George's shoes made a clatter. It could not be helped, and they were nearly at the end now. All Agatha wanted was to find her mother and father again. It did not seem to matter now whether they were still being hunted or not. Down they went, faster and faster, on to the next landing, down another flight and on to the one below. There seemed no end to the stairs.

'See, we were right at the top,' Agatha explained to George. 'The lift man said so.'

It was a long, long way down, and when they came to the bottom of the last flight Agatha gasped and stood motionless. The place they had arrived at did not look

like a shop at all. It was a great, half-lit vault of a place, smelling of car exhausts. The floor was of concrete with patches of black oil on it. One car was parked near them and as they arrived the tail light of another was just disappearing round a dark corner. The sound of its engine echoed from wall to wall. On the other side of the wide expanse of floor was a big opening, dimly lit. Perhaps it led up to the shop again.

'Come on,' said Agatha. 'Quick.'

'I don't like it here,' said George as she rushed him towards it.

It was a kind of tunnel, sloping gently upward. The smell of it told them that it was often used by motor cars or lorries. At the far end there seemed to be more lights, and thinking this was the ground floor at last, Agatha began to run. She could hear George panting beside her.

They were quite a long way up the tunnel when they heard a queer, rumbling noise. It seemed to come from all round them. George suddenly pulled back and Agatha saw that he was staring upwards. She looked upward too; something was beginning to come down from the ceiling. For a minute they were both too frightened to move, and as they watched, a huge, black sliding door came slowly down before them until it reached the ground. It made a small bumping sound as it stopped. They were now faced with a solid wall, blocking the entire tunnel. Across it in big letters Agatha was able to read the words, FIRE CURTAIN.

It was too much for George. He pulled back and began to bawl loudly. There was nowhere to go but back, and they turned and ran for dear life back to the stairs. They clattered up the first flight, not caring how much noise they made, only bent on getting out of that dark, enormous cave below. They stopped, panting, on the second landing. Light and something else was pouring into it from the entrance to that floor. Agatha sniffed. Among other foody smells was that familiar, welcome smell of roasting chicken.

'We're here,' she said breathlessly to George. 'We're back in the Food Hall.' Together they burst into the light, not caring any longer who might see them. But there was no one about. In a far corner the cleaners were still busy and they could hear the sound of the vacuum cleaners. But the passages between the counters and shelves of food were empty of people. No one saw them at all as they hurried across to the roasting chicken counter where their mother and father would be waiting for them.

Agatha had no trouble in finding it. She came upon it almost before she expected, because there were no people round it now. The lights that showed you the

chickens turning and roasting on the spit were out. The chickens were no longer turning, and all that remained was the lingering smell of roasting birds. There was no longer a white-coated person behind the counter. Worst of all, there was no one – no one at all – waiting beside the chickens for two children to turn up.

Chapter Five

IT took her a long time to realize that the floor was empty of all but the cleaners. It was night time. The chickens had been put away, the spit turned off and everyone gone home. Mr and Mrs Pepper had gone home too.

George had been smelling the remains of the cooking smells and now he said loudly, 'I'm hungry.'

At first Agatha could think of nothing but that her mother and father had gone home, leaving them behind. She could not believe it and began hunting round the other counters in case they should be there still. But they weren't, and at last she had to realize that they had, indeed, left without their children. She would not have believed it possible. A terribly lost, hollow feeling started to creep up from the middle of her stomach. It made her cold all over, and shivery. It was George saying again that he was hungry that made her remember that she was nine. She must still look after George – more than ever, now he had no one but her. And it was still her fault that they were here. She began to wonder if her mother and father had been so angry that they could no longer bear the sight of her. Perhaps this was why they had left. A tear trickled down her cheek and bounced on to the chicken counter.

George had been looking round at all the food that still lay piled up on the counters. But now he pulled at her hand and turned to look at her. She took a great breath, swallowed, and quickly wiped her wet cheek on her sleeve.

'Well, if you're hungry we must find you something lovely to eat, mustn't we? There's plenty here.'

George's face had been an alarming mixture of anger, greed and fear. But now it was suddenly transformed by a wide and sunny smile.

'Goody,' he said. 'There's cakes.'

'Come on then,' said Agatha. 'We'll see what we can find and you shall eat as much as you want.' Now that George had no one but her, she had to take the risk that it might be stealing. It was her fault he was hungry and without parents, and she would give him as much to eat as she was able.

In the end it was George's stomach that was not able. They had found their way in among the cakes. All the glass cases were open at the back and there were plenty for them to choose from. There were all kinds – sponge, cinnamon, chocolate, caramel, strawberry, nut. Most of them were filled with a kind of cream that both of them thought the loveliest thing they had ever tasted until about the third cake. When they had finished that they decided they would never eat that sort of cream again.

There was plenty more to eat on other counters – cheese, fruit, biscuits and endless boxes of chocolates. But none of it looked as delicious as it had before. George, his mouth wreathed with chocolate, was quiet and dreamy. Agatha knew that they must now leave the shop and try to find Wynyard Station. Someone would tell them which train to catch. Someone would have to tell them the way to Wynyard Station, too. After that she knew the way home. And, more important, she knew the way out from the Food Hall.

'Come on, Georgie,' she said. 'We'll go home now.'

They walked hand in hand up the wide stairs to the doorway where they had come in. She pushed first one door and then another. She pushed all the doors in turn, but none would open. She was just trying to remember how to find her way to the side door, which she knew was somewhere there, when George said, 'I feel sick.'

'Don't be silly, George. It's just because you're tired.' It was what her mother had sometimes said. But she looked at George's face and saw that all the red had gone from his cheeks. They were now a yellowy-green

colour. 'Come on then. Quick,' she said. 'And don't be
sick until I get you to the bathroom.'

She knew where it was – up the stairs for several
flights and into the door on the landing.

They got there just in time. George was sick in a very
lavish way while Agatha held him. When she had

finally got him mopped up he yawned, shivered and started to cry with a high, mewing sound like a kitten. He seemed to have crumpled and gone strangely bendy. It was no use trying to get him to Wynyard Station in the state he was in now. He yawned again, between sobs. It was his bedtime. It was at this moment that Agatha had her brainwave.

'I know where you'll be as warm and cosy as anything. I'll show you.' She led him out of the bathroom, across the stairway and out on to the floor. They had only just stepped round behind a big refrigerator when they heard voices. They stayed where they were while the cleaners went past. The cleaning of this floor had been done and the cleaners were on their way to another floor. For a moment Agatha thought of asking them to help. But she remembered the cakes they had eaten and the woman who had wanted to charge their parents, and she did not. When the footsteps and voices had died away down the stairs Agatha led George on towards the far end of the building. It was much darker now, for most of the lights were out. But she was able to find her way to what she was looking for.

Side by side, looking very comfortable and inviting were two white beds. They were both covered with heavy, brightly-coloured counterpanes. She pulled one back. There was the pillow, waiting for a head. There were no sheets, but the mattress looked very soft. She pulled the counterpane farther back, scooped George up behind the knees and dropped him on the bed. He gave a great sigh and snuggled in at once. She pulled the

counterpane up under his chin. Then she stood and looked round. The cleaners had gone, but they might come back. She pulled the counterpane farther up still. George could still breathe, she thought, but in that dark corner of the floor he might not have been there at all. She thought he was almost asleep. But when she tried to step back his eyes flew open and he clutched her hand.

'Don't go,' said George, and his fingers closed over hers – tight.

She had meant to leave him there while she looked for a door out of the building. But she would have to wait now until he was properly asleep. The second bed was right beside George's. She loosened his fingers, whispered in his ear and crawled quickly into it. As she pulled the counterpane up over her head she took one last look at George. His eyes were closed, but a satisfied smile flickered round his still chocolaty mouth. She settled herself to wait until it was safe to move. After all the events of the day it was nice to lie down, no matter where, in the quiet and the dark and the warmth. Before long her eyes closed too and she began to breathe with a slow, deep rhythm. No one would have guessed that in that shadowy corner of the empty floor there was a child asleep in each of the two white beds.

Chapter Six

MR PEPPER was late getting home. Mrs Pepper had had the dinner ready for quite a long time. She met him at the door and said at once, 'It's a long time after the children's bedtime. I wondered where you were.'

'Why didn't you put them to bed? They didn't have to stay up for me.' He was still rather cross because taking the day off had made it necessary for him to work late.

'Don't be silly,' said Mrs Pepper. 'How could I, when they were with you?'

It was then that Mr Pepper forgot to be cross. He looked at Mrs Pepper hard and said, 'But I haven't got them. You brought them home.'

Then Mrs Pepper stopped being cross, too. Their faces grew quite white and they both started talking at once. Mrs Pepper started to shake and in the end Mr Pepper put his arm round her and they went together to the telephone to ring up the police.

Chapter Seven

AGATHA woke up some time later, remembered after a minute or so where she was and looked at George. He was buried beneath the counterpane, but she could tell by his breathing that he was fast asleep. She slid quietly out of her bed and pulled the counterpane up over the pillow. There was no sound of cleaners now and she made her way towards the stairs. The shadows seemed to follow her. She stopped. If George woke and found she had gone he would be frightened. He never liked being alone in the dark, and the only lights were now down near the lifts and the motionless escalators. It would be better if she could put on a light near George. She went over to the wall and in the gloom began to feel about for a switch. She had to feel about what seemed to be piles of large metal boxes. It was sheer luck that made her hand fall on the only switch there was. She clicked it on.

Nothing happened. She stepped back to see if a light had come on anywhere near George's bed. She was standing half turned from the wall when out of the

corner of her eye she saw something move. She spun back towards the wall. There was no sound, but she sprang backwards, clapping both hands over her mouth to smother the scream that grew like a bubble inside her. Facing her the heads of twenty furious men with blue shirts and red hair were shouting silently. She saw their lips move. She saw their teeth clenched in fury and she would have run for her life, but she found she could not take one step. She could not shift her eyes from the twenty angry faces, all looking straight at her. Then, as she watched, all the faces faded. Instead, twenty placid rivers flowed beneath twenty drooping green willows and a yellow sun gleamed across the water. Her knees gave way and she found herself sitting, her heart beating wildly, in front of twenty colour television sets.

When she had control of herself again she went to the wall, found the switch and turned it off. The television sets faded into darkness. How awful it would have been, she thought, if the sound had been turned on too.

She did not try any more to find a light for George, but went quickly downstairs. The whole store was absolutely silent now. There was no sound of cleaners at all. They must all have gone home, and she was sorry, because she had decided she would, after all, have asked them to help. She had begun to think that being caught when George fell into the honey would have been better than the terrible loneliness of the empty store.

Chapter Eight

THERE were very few lights anywhere now. As she went down flight after flight of resting escalators she could see the loaded counters and tables. Sometimes it was crockery and china, pots and pans. Sometimes it was suitcases and travelling bags and folded stacks of tartan rugs. Once she jumped back quickly as she went from one escalator to another. She had bumped into a person wearing a cap and a windjacket. But it was only a model posed in a lifelike position on a low table. She told herself sternly not to be frightened. The only person she would see now would be a burglar and she did not expect to find one in the middle of David Jones.

On one floor she found herself walking past bicycles, tricycles and scooters. She had always wanted a scooter. There was one with red handlebars and shining metal wheels just beside her. From where she was standing there was a clear space down the whole length of the store. The end was lost in shadows, but there was not a soul about and not a sound. It would only take a minute. She put one hand on the red handlebars. They

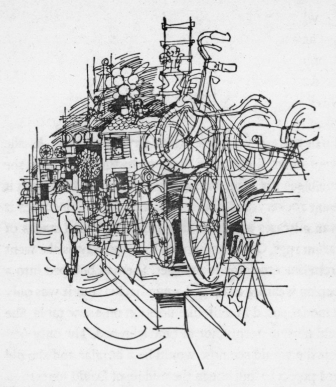

had a nice, shiny feel. She pulled gently. As if it had
been waiting the scooter rolled smoothly towards her.
She put her other hand on the handlebars, stepped on to
the platform with her right foot and gave one quick
push on the floor with the other. She found herself
gliding down the open space. It was so easy, so smooth.
She pushed again and the scooter sprang obediently
forward. She was spinning down the store, her hair lift-

ing with the passing air. She only meant to go to the end and back. For the first time since she had pushed George into the honey she felt happy. On she went into the darkness. Something loomed up in front of her. She never saw what it was, but Agatha and the scooter came to a sudden stop. There was a crash and things began falling on her head. They were sharp, heavy things, and they not only hurt her head, but made a terrible noise when they landed on the floor. In the silent store the sound was like thunder.

In a panic she scrambled out from the mess and the fallen scooter and ran back to the escalators. Panting and frightened, she clattered down flight after flight until she came to the ground floor. There was the side door. Through it she could see the reflection of the traffic lights changing from red to green. Cars began to move past in the street outside. She hurried to the door and pushed. Then she pulled. The side door was locked too.

The street looked so near – just the other side of the glass. A man and a woman walked past laughing together. She thought of attracting their attention, but they had disappeared, and it was too late. If there was no way out, she thought with a touch of panic, she and George would have to hide in the shop till daytime. But there must be a way. There, in the corner, were the stairs, and she walked towards them. She found that now there were places on the far side of the stairs, in the same position as the bathroom above that she had not noticed before. There were cupboards and shelves and piles of big cartons. There were several enormous square wicker baskets on wheels, standing about on the concrete floor. Surely among all this there must be a door somewhere. She was creeping quietly now, for the noise she had made with the scooter had nearly frightened her out of her wits.

It had startled the only other person in the store, too. He did not expect to hear noises in the store at the dead of night. He cautiously pulled a torch from his pocket and set off to investigate. He had already been round the whole building once since the cleaners had left some time after ten-thirty. Everything had been quiet then. He had investigated every floor and he could have sworn everything was as he had hoped to find it. He had not intended to do anything more for another hour. But there had distinctly been a noise where he did not expect a noise. He left his position, climbed the stairs two at a time and slipped in behind the shopping part of the store, intending to come quietly out at the other side – unexpectedly.

Agatha was half way along and had been looking into one of the big baskets. She saw the man's shadow

as he crossed the landing. Her heart gave an extra big
beat and without thinking she stepped on a carton and
jumped into the basket. Crouched on the floor of it
among some empty wrappings she was almost im-
possible to see. The man was walking very quietly, but
he was coming towards her and she could hear the
swish of his rubber soles on the concrete. She stopped

breathing, knew that he was beside her huddled in the corner of the basket, and almost cried out as he gave it a push. She and the basket bumped against the wall, and she heard the quiet feet going on to the far end.

She waited in the basket a long time, not daring to make a move. The feet had been so furtive, his going and coming had been so quiet that she was sure it must be a burglar. She wondered if he would go to the top floor, and if he did, whether he would notice the slight rise in the counterpane on the little white bed. It was more necessary than ever that she should find a way out. After what seemed a very long time she raised her head and looked over the rim of the basket. The place was empty. There was no sound. She climbed out.

Chapter Nine

SHE went downstairs again, this time investigating
every opening she came to on the far side of the stairs.
She came at last to the desk that the man had just left.
Beyond it in the very corner of the building was a
flight of steps and a big door. It was one she had not
seen before, for it was the one the staff used. She rushed
towards it and felt for the handle. It turned, but the
door did not open. She could not unlock it either, for
the man had locked it and taken the key. Sadly she
turned back towards the desk. She did not notice a half-
finished cup of tea. But she noticed a telephone. With
a gasp of thankfulness she rushed towards it and
picked up the receiver.

Before she had thought about dialling, a voice said
in her ear, 'Yes? Anything wrong?'

'Yes. Oh, yes,' she said. 'Yes, there is. Please – oh,
please come quickly.'

Whoever was at the other end seemed to know the
sound of fear when he heard it. He said, 'O.K. love,
we'll be there. Don't panic now. Just a couple of

minutes.' She put the receiver down thankfully. She had spoken to a person at last – a kind person. And she felt better.

The next thing was to get back to George before he woke up. Before the burglar discovered him. She found her way back to the ground floor. There was the row of lifts, all waiting with their doors open. It would be quicker in the lift and she would not risk running into the burglar. She stepped into the first one and pushed the button to the top floor. Nothing happened. She pushed it again. Still nothing happened. So she got into the next lift – and the next. None of them was working.

She had to decide whether it would be better to go up the stairs or the escalators. If there was anyone on the floor, busy stealing the goods, she would not be noticed on the stairs. On the other hand the burglar might use the stairs himself. Suppose she suddenly came face to face with him? She would never get away. In the escalator she could see all round and she could crouch out of sight if she saw anyone. She could not see anyone moving on the ground floor, so she crept towards the escalators. She began to climb very slowly, very silently, on all fours. Now and then she looked over the rail. Nobody.

By this time the man had got to the third floor. So

far he had seen nothing unusual. But there had been a noise and he was determined to find out where it had come from. As Agatha reached the first floor and stopped to look and listen, he came upon the scooter. He flashed his torch around and saw that it was lying in a heap of toy building blocks. They were all sizes and shapes, some wooden, some metal and some plastic. Their boxes had been broken in the fall and they were lying about in a terrible mess.

The man could not think how they, or the scooter, came to be there. It seemed that the scooter had run into the stand, and perhaps in the dark that might have happened. Children in the shop might have done it. Mothers were terrible about not looking after their children when they went shopping. But the cleaners would have found it and tidied it all up. They would never have left such a mess. He stood and scratched his head.

At the same time Agatha was having a brainwave. As she stood peering round the shadowed corners of the first floor she remembered that there was a door leading out into Centrepoint. This, surely, would be open. But now there was menace in the shadows all over the place. She did not much like the idea of crossing the whole floor. That man was a quiet mover and he could be busy stealing somewhere – quietly. Again she

thought of George and heard her father's words, 'You're nine now.' Creeping from counter to counter, past rows of shining leather shoes, smelling the leather and the faint suggestion of mothballs, brushing past

garments she could only dimly see, she reached the door to Centrepoint. The passage beyond was dark, and below she could see the moving car lights in the street. But the door was locked. She and George would after all have to hide from the burglar till daytime.

Chapter Ten

THE journey back to the escalator seemed even longer. But it was not so frightening, for she was now fairly sure there was no one on the First Floor. This meant the man must be higher – nearer to George. Up she went, on all fours again. The stairs hurt her knees. She did not stop to see whether he was on the second floor, but crawled round to the next set of escalators and went on up.

She reached the Third Floor just as the man came up with the scooter. He was putting it quietly back, out of the way. Agatha saw the beam of the torch – a long, wavering streak of bright light. It was coming towards her. Then she heard the footsteps as well. She had just stepped on to the floor from the escalator, but now she froze. To go up meant that sooner or later the torch would be sure to shine on her. She began very slowly to back away to the escalator she had just climbed. But the torch, wavering about as the man steered the scooter, caught her head and shoulders. Her shadow,

moving, fell sharply on the floor in front of her. At once the torch became still.

'Who's there?' said the man.

Agatha had never heard a burglar's voice before. She was rather surprised that it should sound so commanding. In a panic she left the stairs and flew round the corner. There was a crash as the man dropped the scooter. With the torch beam waving in front of him he rushed into the open space between the escalators and the lifts. He was no longer quiet. His feet were thumping and his breathing, not far below her, was easy to hear.

For the moment Agatha was out of the torch beam. But the man had turned round the end of the escalators and was coming her way. In a minute she would be in the beam, and her legs were not nearly as long as his. At her shoulder on the top of a shelf stood a dummy. It was the size of someone like herself and it was wearing what looked like trousers. Agatha was wearing woollen trousers too. Just beyond the dummy the top of the shelf was empty. She clawed her way up to it, balanced herself and took up a pose as near to the dummy's as she could manage. She was only just in time. Underneath her the torch beam flashed along the open space. Behind the torch in the black darkness beyond the beam came what she thought was a burglar.

She held her breath, hoping he would not flash the torch upwards. If he had he would have seen that one dummy had hair made out of a floor mop. The other, though just as motionless, had real hair.

All the man saw was two dummies where he had expected to find them. He did not look up but went crashing on down the floor. It was his job to catch intruders and the sooner he caught this one the better. He did not think this one could get out of the shop. The doors were locked and he had checked all the windows only two hours ago. The fellow must have stayed behind, concealed somewhere after closing time. On he went, flashing his torch.

Agatha climbed very carefully down from the shelf. He would be coming back in a minute, but she might just have time to reach the upward escalator. Then she would be safe unless he happened to shine the torch directly up the steps. She ran as quietly as she could. He was still at the far end as she started to climb. Half way up she stopped and looked quickly and cautiously over the hand rail. He was coming back down the floor. She must get to the top and on to George before he decided to check the escalator.

She had just reached the top step and was almost out of range of the torch when a sound in the street outside made her stop. She heard it again, growing louder.

It was only the sound of a fire engine. She was about
to go on up when there was a shout from the foot of
the escalators. She had paused just a fraction too long
and now she was clear in the torchlight.

'Don't you move a step. You wait there,' shouted a
terrible voice from below.

The man's feet began to pound on the stairs. She

turned and made for the upward escalator. There was nothing for it now but speed. If she could get to the top of that flight in time he might think she had stopped on the next floor. He might stop and look for her. On she went, forcing her legs up the long climb. Although she did not know it, she was making gasping, wheezing noises as she breathed.

Chapter Eleven

FAR away on the other side of the Harbour, half way up the North Shore Line her father was talking to a policeman on the telephone again. The policeman was saying, 'Not yet, Mr Pepper, but don't worry. We'll find them before long. There was no point wasting time looking in the Market Street store the way Mrs Pepper wanted. If they were there they'd have been found by the nightwatchman. They always have one on duty there. If you say your daughter could give him your phone number you'd have heard from him by now. We'll keep on looking, Mr Pepper. All right, if you insist we'll send a man along there, but all he'll do is talk to the nightwatchman. Be in touch, Mr Pepper.'

Chapter Twelve

AGATHA reached the final flight of the escalator just in time. She was going much more slowly now. This was the time she had to be quiet, but it was hard to breathe quietly any more. If he would only think she had stayed on the floor below she might get to George before the burglar found him. She had not thought what to do after that. As she started up the stairs she saw a glass flower vase standing beside the escalators. It was gleaming very faintly in the dim light. She picked it up by the neck and threw it as far as she could across the shop. In the absolute silence the crash sounded like a major explosion. As Agatha crouched on the fourth step, the man came pounding past the escalators from the floor below. He was shouting, 'You stop there at once. Do you hear me? You'll be in real trouble if you don't.'

At the top of the escalators Agatha had to stop and get her breath before she could go another step. She was on the top floor now. In one minute she would be with George. She looked round for something to de-

fend him with if necessary. A folded beach umbrella
was lying beside an inflated plastic pool almost at her
feet. She picked it up. It was rather heavy, but it would
do until she could find something else. She began to
walk softly to the far side of the floor. The shadows hid
her fairly well. Out of reach of the torch she felt safer.
She could hear the man still pounding about on the

floor below. She had decided he must be a very strange burglar to be so determined to find her. She tried not to think what he might do if he caught her or George.

She was half way to the pair of little white beds when she heard the man's footsteps grow louder. He was walking towards the escalators again. She hoped he would think she had escaped and gone downstairs again.

This was exactly what he did think, and he had one foot on the downward step when a terrible thing happened. From the far end of the top floor came a sudden loud wail. It changed to a terrified roaring as George realized he was alone in the dark in a strange place.

Far below on the ground floor a bell rang at the same time. But no bell was a match for George and neither Agatha nor the man heard it. But the man had heard George. He could not have helped hearing George and now he came up the stairs two at a time. Agatha rushed forward shouting, 'It's all right, George. I'm here.' She could see a small, dim figure standing on the bed. It looked too small to be making so much noise. She ran up to him, dropped the beach umbrella and clasped her arms round him. He still felt very warm, but his face was wet and his mouth wide open. She put her hand over it. A strangled sound vibrated through her fingers. She pulled him off the bed, hugging him

and kissing his sodden cheek. Behind her she could hear the running footsteps. When she swept him off his feet and pushed him under the bed he was too surprised to protest. She snatched up the beach umbrella. Holding it in front of her she jumped down to face the approaching man. She could see nothing but the bright torch beam, but as it drew near she lunged forward with the point of the umbrella.

'You keep away,' she heard herself shouting.

Strangely, that was just what happened. The man was so surprised to see someone as young as Agatha that he stopped right where he was. The torch beam sank to her feet. Now she could see the figure of the man outlined behind it and she swung the umbrella in a great circle.

'Keep away,' she shouted again.

Unfortunately the latch on the umbrella was not firmly fixed. The umbrella flew open and the man almost fell backwards as he was faced with a swirling parachute of red and yellow stripes.

'Now, now,' he said when he could find his voice. 'There's no need for that.'

'Keep away,' said Agatha. 'Keep away, or I'll stick it right into you.'

But the beach umbrella was not nearly such a good weapon when it was wide open and now the man began to walk forward. Before Agatha could stop him he had grasped the umbrella by the point and pulled it to one side. Another sharp pull and it flew out of Agatha's hand, away, and over into the television department.

So far Agatha still thought she was dealing with a burglar. Her weapon was gone and George from

beneath the bed was beginning to make more loud
noises. Screaming, she flew at the man, feet kicking,
finger nails aimed at his face. Nine is a good deal older
than four, but it is just not big enough for forty-seven,
and in spite of all her efforts Agatha found herself
caught, held down and helpless. But she could still kick
and she did.

'Ouch!' said the man.

'Let me go,' shouted Agatha. But her voice was muffled because her face was pressed into the man's middle.

'You stop kicking and I'll let you go,' said the man. 'Easy now. Come on.'

The voice had a kinder tone than Agatha had expected. She stopped wriggling.

'There now,' said the man, whose shins were still tingling. 'Steady on. Did you think I was going to eat you?'

Before Agatha could think of anything to say George let out another wail from beneath the bed.

'How many more,' said the man, 'are there under that bed?' His grasp on Agatha slackened and she wriggled free. Now she saw him close to he did not look as savage as she had expected.

'It's only my brother,' she said. 'You leave him alone.'

'I wasn't going to hurt him,' said the man. 'What I want to know is – what are you both doing here?'

Agatha looked up into his face. It seemed to be an ordinary kind of face. She might have been conquered, but she was not yet defeated. 'What are *you* doing here?' she said. 'Are you a burglar?'

'A burglar?' The man sounded quite horrified. 'Of course I'm not a burglar. I'm the nightwatchman. I'm here to look after the store.'

For a long time Agatha looked at him in silence. She could feel the fight and the fear draining out of her. Then she said in a humble voice, 'Could you – could you look after us, too? See, we – I – that is, I pushed

George in the honey and when we'd got it washed off and everything Mummy and Daddy had gone home. They went away without us.' She swallowed quickly because there had been a wobble in her voice at the end. But she held her head high. 'I'll fetch George now,' she said, and turned and went to the bed.

George had crawled out and was standing beside it not knowing whether to go forward. She led him by the hand towards the nightwatchman. But the night-watchman had turned round and now stood with his back to them, listening. There seemed, all of a sudden, to be a lot of noise coming from somewhere down-stairs. Men were shouting, whistles were blowing and there was a sound of tramping feet.

'You kids stay here,' said the nightwatchman quickly. 'Don't move. I'll be back.' He left them, run-ning for the stairs in the corner and disappeared quickly into the darkness.

Chapter Thirteen

AGATHA led George back to the bed and they sat down together to wait. She put the counterpane round him to keep him warm. They sat there for what seemed like a long time. Then there were feet again, and voices. Suddenly all the lights on the floor went on. Agatha and George blinked. Several men were coming towards them. Agatha thought it was a bit like a fancy dress party. First there was the nightwatchman, and in the clear light his face was not a bit frightening. Then there was a policeman in uniform and behind him two men from the fire brigade with their helmets gleaming under the lights.

Agatha took a firmer grip of George. They both watched in silence as the men came nearer. George's mouth began to fall open. When the men reached them they stood in a stern line, all looking at the two figures on the bed. Agatha had just begun to think it would have been nice to be a few years older than nine, and bigger, too, when the nightwatchman spoke.

'I've just found them. They must have been here

since closing time. Can't think why they weren't found before by the cleaners.'

One of the firemen now took a step forward, bent at the knees and looked into Agatha's face. 'Little girl, did you ring up on the telephone downstairs about twenty minutes ago?'

Agatha nodded. She could not speak. The fireman stood up and looked at the other men. 'That's it, then. It was a child's voice. She'd hung up before I could ask any details.'

The nightwatchman seemed to be unhappy about something, and now he said to the fireman, 'You didn't have to break the glass to get in. You could have rung the bell.'

'We did,' said the fireman. 'But you were all over the shop chasing children. We'd have waited only the little girl sounded so frightened.'

They all looked at Agatha now and she could feel her face going red. The nightwatchman suddenly stepped forward and put his hand on her shoulder. 'Don't worry, love,' he said unexpectedly. 'You weren't to know it was the direct line to the fire brigade.'

The policeman now cleared his throat and came forward too. 'Would your name be Agatha Pepper?' he asked. Standing before her, tall and blue and solemn, he looked very alarming indeed. Agatha could only nod once more. 'That's it then,' said the policeman. 'I'd better let the Station know and they'll get the parents to come and collect them.'

'We'd better all go down to my desk,' said the nightwatchman. 'You can use the phone there.' Agatha felt her hand grasped by his own large, hard, warm one. He would have pulled her up, but she clutched George more tightly.

'I'll carry this fella,' said one of the firemen.

As he bent to scoop George into his arms, George looked up into his face and said, 'I been sick.'

The fireman took a step back, but Agatha said quickly, 'It's all right. I mopped him up.'

They all went down the concrete stairs to the nightwatchman's desk. In the dark and empty building they sounded like an army. The policeman went straight to the telephone and they heard him talking briskly. He put down the receiver and said, 'That's O.K. The Station will let their father know and they'll be along to collect them straight away. They'll be all right here, will they?'

The nightwatchman nodded. 'Another half hour or so before I go on me next round won't make much difference, I suppose.'

When the two firemen and the policeman had gone and the nightwatchman had locked the door behind

them he turned to Agatha and George. 'I could make
you a nice cup of cocoa. I got some here. You could
drink it while you're waiting.'

Agatha nodded. Now that it was all over she was
almost too tired to speak. But she did not want to seem
ungrateful. The nightwatchman had been kind. 'George
and me would like it, thank you,' she said at last.

The nightwatchman had some too. 'Soon as your
parents come I'll have to see about that broken

window,' he said. 'But I won't leave you alone.'

They waited for a time in silence, the nightwatchman humming gently to himself. When she had finished her cocoa Agatha said, 'There's a big cave underneath and a sort of tunnel. And a wall comes out of the roof. It says FIRE CURTAIN, but it isn't a curtain at all.'

'You mean you've been all the way down to the basement?' said the nightwatchman in surprise.

'If that place is the basement we have,' said Agatha. 'We didn't mean to.'

'That's the tunnel to the other shop,' said the nightwatchman. 'It goes under the street. They put that curtain down every night just in case a fire in one shop might spread to the other. Fancy your finding your way right down there.'

It seemed a long time till Mr and Mrs Pepper came. But at last a bell shrilled near them. Agatha and George both jumped, and George dropped his mug.

'Good thing it was empty,' said the nightwatchman. 'Wait here now while I open the door.' He left his desk and walked round the corner to the big doors. They heard the bolt click back. The door gave a small squeak and there came the sound of voices.

Agatha slipped off her chair and walked slowly round the corner of the desk. She stood waiting, her eyes wide open and bruised with tiredness. The foot-steps came nearer and the voices grew louder – familiar voices. Then she saw her mother and father come into the light. He had his arm round her and seemed to be looking after her just as Agatha had tried to look after George. She looked at them both and said, 'You left us. You went away without us.' She stood up very straight and shut her lips tight.

'We didn't mean to,' said Mrs Pepper. 'Agatha, we didn't mean to. It was all a horrid muddle. But it will never happen again.' She took a step forward and Agatha suddenly rushed towards her. She pushed her face hard into Mrs Pepper's coat so that no one could see the shameful tears.

'Take them home,' said the nightwatchman. 'They're that tired. She's been a brave girl. I'd be proud of her if she was mine.'

MR BERRY'S ICE-CREAM PARLOUR
Jennifer Zabel

Carl is thrilled when Mr Berry the new lodger comes to stay. But when Mr Berry announces his plan to open an ice-cream parlour, Carl can hardly believe it. And this is just the start of the excitements in store when Mr Berry walks through the door!

THE PICTURE PRIZE
Simon Watson

An enchanting collection of fresh and amusing stories about mischievous Wallace and his younger brother, Henry. From unexpected pony rides, to collecting caterpillars, to losing a tooth, it's clear that everyday incidents become real adventures when Wallace is around.

THE DISAPPEARING CAT and NO SWIMMING FOR SAM
Thelma Lambert

Appearing together in one volume for the first time are these two stories about school life.

ONE NIL
Tony Bradman

Dave Brown is mad about football and when he learns that the England squad are to train at the local City ground he thinks up a brilliant plan to overcome his parents' objections and get him to the ground to see them.

ON THE NIGHT WATCH
Hannah Cole

A group of children and their parents occupy their tiny school in an effort to prevent its closure.

FIONA FINDS HER TONGUE
Diana Hendry

At home Fiona is a chatterbox but whenever she goes out she just won't say a word. How she overcomes her shyness and 'finds her tongue' is told in this charming book.

IT'S TOO FRIGHTENING FOR ME!
Shirley Hughes

The eerie old house gives Jim and Arthur the creeps. But somehow they just can't resist poking around it, even when a mysterious white face appears at the window! A deliciously scary story – for brave readers only!

THE CONKER AS HARD AS A DIAMOND
Chris Powling

Last conker season Little Alpesh had lost every single game! But this year it's going to be different and he's going to be Conker Champion of the Universe! The trouble is, only a conker as hard as a diamond will make it possible – and where on earth is he going to find one?

THE GHOST AT NO. 13

Giles Brandreth

Hamlet Brown's sister, Susan, is just too perfect. Everything she does is praised and Hamlet is in despair – until a ghost comes to stay for a holiday and helps him to find an exciting idea for his school project!

RADIO DETECTIVE

John Escott

A piece of amazing deduction by the Roundbay Radio Detective when Donald, the radio's young presenter, solves a mystery but finds out more than anyone expects.

RAGDOLLY ANNA'S CIRCUS

Jean Kenward

Made only from a morsel of this and a tatter of that, Ragdolly Anna is a very special doll and the six stories in this book are all about her adventures.

SEE YOU AT THE MATCH

Margaret Joy

Six delightful stories about football. Whether spectator, player, winner or loser these short, easy stories for young readers are a must for all football fans.